The Little Drummer Girl of Gettysburg

By

Ed Kelemen

Disclaimer

This novel is a work of fiction. Names, characters, and incidents depicted in this book are the product of the author's imagination or are used fictitiously Any resemblance to actual events, locales, organizations, or persons, living or dead is entirely coincidental and beyond the intent of the author or the publisher.

Published in the United States of America by
Nemeleke Publishing
New Florence, PA
March 2013

DEDICATION

This book is dedicated to my father, Ed S. Kelemen who gave me my love of reading and to my son, Erik Kelemen who gave me my love of Gettysburg.

TABLE OF CONTENTS

ACKNOWLEDGMENTS

This book would have been impossible without the assistance, patient input, and encouragement of the members of the Greensburg Writers Group. To single out individual members for their insight, assistance, editing, gentle critique, and steadfast attention to continuity would be a disservice to all the other members of the group. All I can do is express my gratitude for all their unselfish help.

The cover art is another example of the exemplary work done by Linda Ciletti. You can visit with her at www.lindaciletti.net.

Special thanks goes to Judith Gallagher of Gallagher Editorial Services for her proof-reading assistance. Any typos, misspellings, or grammatical errors found in this book are the results of gremlins who invaded these pages *after* she made all the corrections.

-Prologue-

A blistering hot morning on July 1, 1863, on the outskirts of a small farming village in Pennsylvania:

"Run for it, kid!"

"But … but … Ben?"

"No time right now. General Reynolds is dead. Colonels Stone and Wister are both wounded. Colonel Musser is regimental commander, and he says to retreat. Now, git!"

Abigail ran with the coppery taste of fear in her mouth. She tripped over the bodies of her friends, and her feet slipped in their blood. She looked back in both awe and fear. She saw Sergeant Ben slowly retreating, waving the Stars and Stripes, shouting insults and shaking his fist at the advancing Rebels.

Suddenly a rifle volley lifted him off his feet. His lifeless body slammed to the ground of Seminary Ridge. Men of the 143rd Pennsylvania Volunteers ran forward and retrieved the flag, but the withering rifle fire and double-canister shot from the cannons were too much to bear. They fell back, leaving the sergeant's body on the field of battle.

She shouted, "No, no. Ben!" She wanted to go back to help him, but she was caught up in the crush of retreating soldiers rushing to safety and lost track of where she was.

Scuttling up a low stone wall, she paused and looked back through the choking smoke and dust, searching for any sign of Sergeant Ben.

As she turned to face the oncoming Confederates the wind was knocked out of her with what felt like a kick in the chest from a frightened cavalry mount. She flew backwards Blood splattered her drum and uniform, ruining all the work that had gone into polishing buttons and leather for this day.

Abigail lay on her back staring up at the blue sky while men and horses jumped over her, jostling her from time to time.

After a while, a man in a gray uniform looked down on her. She heard him say, "Damn it, he's just a little boy."

Then he took off his backpack, removed a greatcoat from it, and wrapped her up in it. He had carried that coat since his brother had died wearing it at Marye's Heights in Fredricksburg, Virginia two months earlier. The last thing she saw before darkness closed in was the gray cloth he wrapped about her head.

For the next three days, the crash of war swirled about her as the fate of a nation was decided. Hot summer returned to the little farming community that had become famous overnight.

Then death shrouded the field with silence. Eventually she was lowered into the ground. Shovels full of earth thumped down on her.

A long time passed. One day the earth loosened about her and the dirt was brushed from her shroud. She heard someone say, "Look here. It's just another one of them damned traitorous Johnny Rebs. Throw 'im back in."

She screamed, "No! I'm not a rebel. I'm Drummer Boy Abner Russell from Company E of the 143rd Pennsylvania!"

She struggled to free herself from the gray covering the nice man from Virginia had wrapped her in. But she couldn't move. She was dead.

CHAPTER 1

A STOOPID VACATION

A red-faced man in a white hard hat bit on the unlit cigar that was jutting from one side of his mouth and cursed around it.

What was it now? Big Mike wished he'd never signed

on for this job. Hearings, permits, licenses and even a damned class on archaeology. Just so he could repave an intersection in Gettysburg. Every time someone found a musket ball, a scrap of cloth, or a piece of wood in the ground, all construction had to stop while some egghead from the historical society evaluated it. Those prissy idiots with their trowels, brushes, and dental picks acted as though each piece of trash was the tomb of King Tut.

He scratched at a persistent itch under his dirty, sweat-stained T-shirt, climbed up on the treads of the tractor, cupped his hands to make a megaphone and bellowed over the roar, "What is it now, Wally?"

Wally cut the engine, took off his hard hat, and wiped the sweat from his brow. He pointed to a spot in front of the tractor where the hydraulic bucket had uncovered something."I dunno, boss. It looks like a rolled-up rug or something."

Mike climbed down and walked to the ditch in front of the Caterpillar. What looked a piece of gray blanket stuck out of the clayey soil. Mike hunkered down for a closer look. It was a sleeve. Of a Confederate soldier's coat. The rest of the coat was wrapped around something. It was an important archaeological find. It was a major delay in a project already way behind schedule.

"Wally, it's just a damned old rug that someone dumped here. Scoop it up and dump it over there in the tailings pile. We'll use it later for back fill in the drainage ditch."

"But, Mike?"

"No ifs, ands, or buts about it. That rag could hold us up for a week or more. I, for one, ain't gonna tell the bean counters back at the home office that we can't finish the job on time. Besides, there won't be any bonus money unless we're done before the battle anniversary."

"If you say so, Mike," Wally reluctantly restarted the big tractor and angled the bucket to dig out the whole area around the dirt-encased offending item.

"Damn right I say so," mumbled Mike. He stomped back to the field office to see what was going to hold up the project next. He needed that bonus money for an unbreakable promise he had made.

Abby wailed and protested as her body was ignominiously scooped up with two tons of dirt and dumped into the truck that took her to the tailing pile.

Mike paused and looked around as though he heard something. Then he shook his head to clear it and went back to what was knocking around his mind.

Mike was thinking about the vacation that the bonus money would provide for him, his wife, and his little girls. He'd promised the twin eight-year-olds a trip to Walt Disney World. They were the only calm in the turmoil of his life. Nothing was going to make him break that promise.

*

Bert O'Neill stared moodily out the window of the motor home, watching the summer scenery blur past. Round and round, over and over, words ran through his head like a mantra.

Stoopid, boring, lame. Stoopid, boring, lame. Stoopid, boring, lame. This vacation is going to be stoopid, boring, and lame.

At least last year the family had spent their two summer weeks rafting, hiking, fishing, and canoeing in the Adirondacks of New York. Bert was able to forget that his nerdy little pain-in-the-neck sister was with him. She was three whole years younger than his fourteen, and they had nothing in common.

On the way home, they'd spent a day each at Dorney Park and Knoble's Grove, two really great parks with intense roller coasters.

That was how Dad set up a vacation. This year it was Mom's turn. So where did she pick? Gettysburg, that's where. This vacation promised to be a disaster.

Two whole weeks of Mom gushing about Gettysburg and the Civil War was more than he could bear. Just because she was a history teacher didn't mean she had to force all this crap down his throat.

Then there was Emma, Mom's pride and joy.

"If only you'd apply yourself, Bert, then your grades would be as good as Emma's," Mom said.

Perfect little Emma never gets anything but A's, thought Bert. *Smart little Emma always does all her homework correctly, neatly, and on time. Talented little Emma practices the piano for a full hour every day and gives recitals for all the relatives on holidays. Aggravating little Emma is always hanging around, trying to butt in.*

Two long, agonizing weeks trapped in the camper with Emma.

What's there to do at Gettysburg?

"Oh, lots of things," Mom said. "There's blah, blah blah and blah. And at night, they blah, blah, blah."

Bert came to with a start. Was he talking out loud?

With a sigh he realized that Mom was just prattling on to Dad and Emma about what a wonderful time Gettysburg was going to be. Nothing she mentioned sounded like fun.

"And the campground we're staying at has a five-star rating. Fort Wilderness at Walt Disney World has a five-star rating, and you know how great it is. There's a heated pool, a game room, water slides, miniature golf and campfire sing a longs and movies at night."

Well, whoop de doo, Bert thought. *It looks like we're just going to have a grand old time. Yeah, makes me want to puke.*

"And even candlelight ghost tours at night. Gettysburg is said to be one of the most haunted places in America."

Finally Bert's interest was piqued. He had read all of H. P. Lovecraft's and R. L. Stine's horror stories and thought Stephen King almost a god. He devoured books about ghosts, phantoms, and phantasms. "What was that about ghosts, Mom?"

"Well, honey, people say the ghosts of both Confederate and Union soldiers who died during the battle haunt the town and the battlefield. They say that because of the intensity of emotions expended during those three days in July across these rolling farmlands, many of the dead are still here."

Bert turned from the window and asked, "Where'd you hear that, Mom?"

"I read it at the school library. I'm sure we can find many books about the haunting of Gettysburg."

This vacation might not be quite as bad as he'd thought. As long as she didn't mention books again.

CHAPTER 2

DOESN'T EVERYBODY BELIEVE IN GHOSTS?

The next day was Monday.

Mom was awake early enough to wish the birds a good morning before the sun even had time to push the morning damp away. "Up and at 'em. It's after eight," she spouted cheerfully.

Bert groaned and started to pull the sleeping bag up over his head, but delicious smells coming from the little kitchen interrupted that notion. He got into a pair of cutoff jeans and a T-shirt emblazoned with a death's head. He slipped into a pair of old sneakers while rushing to the table. But, as usual, he was the last one to take a seat.

Dad was already sipping from a mug of coffee while Emma sat across from him stuffing her face with French toast dripping with syrup and those little breakfast sausages that everyone liked so much.

Mom put a plate overflowing with food and a glass of orange juice in front of him and said, "Stoke our fires, me hearties. We've got a busy day in front of us."

Oh no, Bert groaned inwardly. *She's starting already.*

Mom sat at the little table with a cup of her favorite herbal tea. She continued, "I figure that today we'll just take a nice walk through the town and see what it has to offer. I hear that there are lots of antique shops. Mary Chastain, the tenth-grade geometry teacher, told me about a quaint little coffee shop that we can stop at when we get tired."

Bert was glad to see that perfect little Emma had a bit of syrup on her chin as she said, "Oh, Mommy, that will be so nice. Can I buy a teacup for my collection?"

Mom reached across with a dampened napkin and wiped Emma's chin. "Of course, dear. I'm sure there will be nice ones in town.

"What's the matter sport?" Dad asked Bert. "You look like you just bit into a lemon."

"N-nothing, Dad. I was just trying to get a piece of sausage from between my teeth." *Geez,* he thought. *Can everybody around here read my mind?*

"Sure enough," piped Emma, startling Bert. Then he realized that she was replying to Mom's request for a hand loading the car.

While Dad and Bert did the dishes, Emma helped Mom load the bikes onto the carrier on the Toad. Toad was what Dad called the old VW Beetle that he dragged behind the motor home.

The kids winced and forced a smile every trip when Dad said, "I call it the Toad. Get it? T-O-W-E-D: Toad." Then Dad laughed at his own joke. No one else would.

Nine o'clock found them on their way the three miles east from the campground to Gettysburg. As soon as they got on the main highway, U.S. 30, Mom started a running commentary. It was like traveling with a tour guide.

Bert endured the morning pretty well, all things considered. He allowed his mind to drift and pretty much ignored Mom. After all, who cared who slept where a hundred and fifty years ago?

Some things managed to grind their way into his memory in spite of himself. Like the fact that the streets were so muddy and full of horse droppings in the 1800s that every building had a little thingy outside the door for scraping boot soles clean. Bert figured that somebody's mom thought of that one.

The foursome walked all over town, going in and out of dusty, musty antique shops that all smelled like the inside of the old trunks in their attic at home.

While Mom and Emma were gushing over pieces of fabric and letters to and from people long dead, Bert dwelt on his boredom and sank deeper into his misery.

By half-past eleven the sun had climbed into the sky

and the preserved nineteenth-century downtown area of Gettysburg was sweltering. Dust motes danced in the sunbeams around the curlicue woodwork of all the old buildings.

"Here's a nice place where we can beat the lunch rush," Mom said, indicating a little café halfway down the block on Baltimore Street.

When the four of them escaped to the air-conditioned room decorated with copies of Union and Confederate battle flags, the conversation naturally turned to the heat of the day.

Dad and Bert both had foreheads shiny with sweat. Dad said something about it being hotter than the hammers of Hades. Bert nodded agreement while a tall glass of cola disappeared through a straw into his mouth, generating slurpy sounds that earned him one of Mom's *looks*.

Emma piped up, "If you think we're hot, just think of all those soldiers during the battle. It was July and they wore woolen trousers and coats cinched around their necks. And they had to carry their rifles, ammunition, and backpacks while running around getting shot at."

After imparting this bit of knowledge to the less informed, she smiled and sipped daintily at her iced tea as though no hot summer day would force her to gulp.

"Geez, Emma," Bert muttered, "that sure makes me feel cooler."

Then the kids' burgers and fries arrived along with the adults' BLTs. Silence descended on the table, interrupted only by the sounds of food being consumed.

When they finished lunch, Dad announced in no uncertain terms that he was through window shopping for the day. "What do you say we all go back to the campground where we can soak in the pool till things cool off?"

Even Emma saw the wisdom in this suggestion. Within an hour, the whole family was comfortable near and in the shade tree surrounded pool.

Bert, liberally slathered with sun-block with a SPF of one million plus, immersed himself up to his neck in the cool water, daydreaming about nothing in particular.

Suddenly he heard a yell. "Cannon Ball!" Next thing he knew a wall of water and foam exploded in the water right beside him.

He stood up, sputtering and shaking water from his eyes and nose.

"What the ...?" he questioned.

When his vision cleared, a freckle-faced girl of about his own age was standing next to him in the water. Her purple and pink hair was plastered to her head, and her blue eyes sparkled impishly. She laughed and said, "I'm sorry. From behind with just your head sticking out of the water I thought you were my little brother. I was trying to get even for something."

"That's OK," Bert mumbled. He climbed out of the water and sat on the edge of the pool with his feet dangling in the water.

The girl pulled herself up, turning in one motion to sit next to Bert.

"Hi. My name's Veronica, but everyone calls me Ronnie. Are you here for the reenactment battle this weekend? My mom and dad made me come because they thought I might learn something. I won't, though. All I'll wind-up doing is babysitting my little brother. I'd rather be riding the Phantom's Revenge at Kennywood Park than tramping around a hot field day after day. I mean, it's sad and all, that so many people died here, but that was ages ago and why should I care now? It's not like I knew them or something, you know?"

She took a breath. Bert took advantage of the pause, "My name's Bert. I'm here with my family, too."

A whoop and a splash were followed by a shriek as Emma disappeared in another cannonball wave, this one courtesy of a stocky sugar-haired imp who clambered out of the water laughing. His laughter was short-lived, however, as Emma ran after him.

As the pair passed Mom and Dad, Mom looked up from her novel and said, "Don't run near the pool, kids."

Emma chased down the tow-headed boy, tackled him, and pinned him to the grass with a hammerlock. She yelled, "Say you're sorry or I'll break your neck."

"OK, OK, I'm sorry," he said. She released her hold on him and he rubbed his neck, "You know, you're pretty strong for a girl."

"You meant to say I'm pretty strong, period. Right?"

He just nodded, her feminism lost on him.

Ronnie shook her head at the younger kids. "I see someone has met my little brother, Derek."

Bert contributed ruefully, "And my little sister, Emma."

A tall, thin, freckled woman with auburn hair, who shared Ronnie and Derek's sparkling blue eyes, introduced herself to Bert's mom and dad. "I see you've met my wrecking crew," she said. "I hope they haven't been too much trouble."

Mrs. O'Neill replied, "No trouble at all. They seem to

hit it off with our kids."

Before Bert even knew what was happening, the Griffins and the O'Neills and learned that they had a shared interest in American history, among other things. The two families made a date for dinner that night.

Josh Griffin (Ronnie and Derek's father) was going to prepare his specialty on the grill: slow-smoked spare-ribs.

The O'Neill' contribution would be Shannon's signature spicy scalloped potatoes, green beans with onions, mushrooms and bacon, and a big tossed salad.

It was suppertime before Bert was even aware of time passing. He was looking forward to dinner. He even wanted to do something about his uncooperative curly dark-brown hair. That was when it dawned on him: his hair was nothing like Derek's from behind or from any other vantage point. *Hmmm.*

The O'Neills walked the short distance to the Griffins' RV, Dad leading the way with the casserole and Bert bringing up the rear with the salad. It was that time a little before sunset when everything gets quiet as the summer afternoon dies and evening takes over.

As soon as they arrived, Bert and Ronnie found themselves squeezing lemons for lemonade while Emma and Derek set the table under the screened awning.

Ronnie and Bert got the usual getting-to-know-you stuff out of the way in short order: where they went to school, favorite subjects, favorite music, favorite sports, most disgusting food, favorite time of the year, and least favorite people.

Ronnie said, "You know, I don't really hate my little brother, but he is just such a pain."

"I know what you mean," replied Bert. "Emma is always underfoot, interrupting me and butting in."

"Derek thinks he's some kind of a commando. Always sneaking up and jumping out at me."

"She's always running around with her iPhone and telling me strange things I don't even want to know."

Then they both said, at the same time, "I wish my little brother/sister would find something to do other than making my life miserable."

"Yeah," said Ronnie, "A real couple of turds in the punchbowl."

They looked at one another, laughed, and exchanged high fives.

Emma and Derek had their heads together, too. Emma was saying, "… and I can download all kinds of apps into my iPhone. Weather forecasts, maps, survival tactics, recipes to survive on if I get lost. I can even make it into a GPS."

Derek's emerald eyes brightened and his platinum blond mop jiggled as he nodded agreement. He said, "Cool," making it sound like "Kew-el."

"Soup's on," yelled Mr. Griffin, "Come 'n get it."

Conversation was limited to what few words could squeeze past the prodigious amounts of ribs, potatoes, beans, and salad that the two families consumed.

Then, just as everyone was mentally pushing away from the table with full-to-bursting stomachs, Ronnie's mother, Heather, went into the RV. She reappeared carrying a tray and announced, "Strawberry shortcake and ice cream."

She was answered with groans. Nevertheless, ten minutes later, there was nary a crumb of shortcake to be found.

After dark, they all gathered around the campfire that they didn't need for warmth, enjoying the end of a day that had seen new friendships forged.

Bert kept looking sideways at Ronnie. She finally noticed it.

"What've you got on – your mind?" she asked.

He didn't want to say something that would make her think he was a loser. He'd done that often enough with other people. But he ramped up his courage anyhow and asked her, "Do you believe in ghosts?"

"Sure. Doesn't everybody?"

Bert turned away to hide his grin.

CHAPTER 3

THE BATTLEFIELD

Tuesday morning found both families exploring the battlefield.

Bert's mom acted as guide since she knew more about Gettysburg than anyone else.

Geez, Bert thought. *I sure hope she doesn't bore everyone to death.*

The small group was standing on the side of the Chambersburg Pike looking across a quiet field of grass and brush that extended a mile or so to the north. Bert thought that it looked like every other piece of farmland he had ever seen.

His mom said, "Imagine on a hot July morning seeing this broad field of green from the back of your spirited war horse. Maybe you cradle a tin of uncomfortably hot coffee in your hands."

She extended her arms out as wide as they would go, then pointed across the fields. "You notice a cloud of dust approaching. You hear squeaks of wheels and clanks of metal upon metal, accompanied by the sound of battle drums and pipers."

Bert glanced at the others. His mom's story held everyone in thrall. Her description was so vivid that they could almost feel quivering horses under them.

She continued, "That's what the members of Union General Buford's cavalry saw that morning. General Buford, knowing that the closest units of the Union Army were four miles the other side of town, ordered his men to get off their horses and take cover behind fences, stumps, rocks, whatever they could find. Their job would be to delay the Confederate Army until General Reynolds could arrive with reinforcements."

Ronnie thought about defenseless animals with bullets singing around them. She asked, "What did they do with the horses?"

Emma spoke up. Pointing toward the building in the distance, she said, "Every fourth man took his horse and three others in the direction of that building with the white dome on top so they would be out of the line of fire."

She held up her iPhone for everyone to see and smugly said, "I downloaded everything about the battle before we left this morning."

Derek faced Bert's mom expectantly and asked, "What happened next?"

"Yes, please go on," Mrs. Griffin added.

Mrs. O'Neill took a sip from her water bottle and said, "Well, the dismounted cavalry held back the rebels until 10:20 in the morning, when they ran out of ammunition and had to fall back. Fortunately General Reynolds and his First Corps Iron Brigade showed up just in time with infantry reinforcements and took over the battlefield from the weary cavalrymen. Let's all go back to the cars and I'll show you what they did."

With the O'Neills in the lead, they drove down the little two-lane road that meandered through the battlefield. They finally circled around to the road they had started on, arriving at a pull-off a couple of hundred yards closer to town.

Mom shepherded everyone to a monument dedicated to the Pennsylvania 143rd Volunteers. It showed a soldier cradling the Stars and Stripes with one arm while waving his other fist at the enemy.

"Right here," she said, "a number of men in Stone's Brigade fought valiantly for hours against overwhelming Confederate forces before falling back through Gettysburg. Many of them died."

She continued, "This chunk of stone was put here in memory of the 143rd Pennsylvanians, who held the center of the line. It shows Color Sergeant Ben Crippen, the regimental flag-bearer, retreating reluctantly and taunting the enemy. He and many men in his regiment had to be forced by their officers to retreat. They were ready to fight to the death.

"He died at just about this spot." Voice breaking, she continued, "He was only five years older than you, Bert."

Bert's dad put his arms around Mom's shoulder and led her back to the car. Mr. and Mrs. Griffin wiped at their eyes and silently went back to their car also, leaving the children at the monument.

"Kew-el," said Derek. "But those guys were braver than they were smart. I'd a dropped the flag and ran"

Ronnie punched him in the shoulder and said, "Shut-up, you dork. People died right where you're standing."

For a change, Emma had nothing to say as she and Bert joined their parents in the toad. The Griffins entered their car silently.

Mom's pretty good at this, Bert thought, listening to her bring the three-day battle to life for the group. She told how the Confederate soldiers had long since run out of supplies, even shoes. They lived off the land, commandeering what supplies were available in the little towns and farms they passed through. It was plundering and looting, but there was no other way they could subsist so far from their home bases more than two hundred miles to the south.

Things were so bad that, even in the heat of battle, the Confederates would stop to strip the boots off dead soldiers. Confederate or Union, it made no difference.

"Believe it or not," she said, "coffee was one of the things Confederate soldiers wanted the most, since the southern United States had run out of it at the beginning of the war. "Union soldiers coveted tobacco, since most of it was grown in the south. In fact, in-between battles the soldiers would trade coffee for tobacco under a sort of a private truce. Then they would go back to killing one another when the officers ordered them to."

The day went pleasantly along until mid-afternoon when the June temperatures soared again. By that time the group, under the tutelage of Bert's mom, had traipsed all through the sites of the first day's battle.

They left the heat of the battlefield and reconvened at the campground's pool, where Bert's dad gave a lesson on how to make really big cannonball splashes off the diving board. "What you need to do," he said, "is to pull one knee up between your hands as your other leg hits the water."

Emma, Bert, Derek, and Ronnie spent the next hour making mini tsunamis in the area of the diving board. The parents wisely moved their umbrella table out of the way of errant splashes.

Bert told Ronnie how much he liked reading spooky stories. She said it was even more fun to write your own.

"Just think how much fun it is to scare someone else with a story you invented yourself," she said.

Meanwhile Emma and Derek had their heads together over Emma's iPhone.

"Look - it can work as a GPS so you never get lost."

"Kew-el."

"I can get weather forecasts on it."

"Kew-el."

"I can even go online and surf the Web with it."

"Kew-el."

"Can't you say anything but 'Kew-el'?

"You know, you're awfully smart - for a girl."

The sound of an open palm hitting the back of a head accompanied that statement. "You mean that I'm smart, period, right?"

"Ow! Yeah. Right."

"Kew-el. Ha-ha."

Before the families separated to go to their respective RVs for dinner, Ronnie and Bert made plans for the next day. She promised to let Bert read some of the scary stories she had written.

After the campfire sing-a-long that evening, Bert went to sleep in his best mood all week.

CHAPTER 4

THE SEANCE

Wednesday morning, Bert's mom had planned on taking everyone to the Devil's Den and Little Round Top.

"Just you guys wait until I show you where the boys from the 20th Maine made a bayonet charge after they ran out of ammunition," she said while wiping the last of the breakfast dishes and handing them to Bert to stow away.

"Uh, Mom?"

"Yes, Bert. What do you want?"

"Ahh, like I don't want to rain on your parade or nothing ... "

"You mean *anything*."

"That's right, Mom. Well, Ronnie and me were talking last night."

Mom interrupted, "Ronnie and *I*."

"Ronnie and I were talking last night."

"That's nice, honey. I'm glad you're making friends here."

Geez, Bert thought, *if she doesn't stop interrupting, I'll never get to ask her.*

He decided to just steam on ahead, talking fast so she couldn't interrupt.

"OK, Mom. What we wanted to know was could we maybe not go into town with you guys? We want to go back where we were yesterday and spend more time where the guys from Pennsylvania fought. We thought we could take our bikes and some food in our backpacks and just let the history of the place soak in. You won't even need to put our bikes on the car since they're still there from Monday."

Bert figured nothing would get his mom's attention like mentioning that he was interested in learning some history. Actually, he and Ronnie planned to just ride their bikes around the battlefield and hang out together without any parents or little brothers or sisters.

Mom brightened. She hung the dish towel on its rack and said, "Let me talk it over with Dad. OK?"

She went outside where Dad was having a cup of coffee. Bert could catch only bits and pieces of their conversation: "He's making new friends," and "Maybe he's starting to mature," and "Do you think he'll be safe?"

Then he heard his dad say, "I'll go over see what the Griffins say about it."

Bert jumped away from the window and tried to look innocent as Mom came inside. "Dad will be back in a couple of minutes with an answer," she told him.

Those couple of minutes seemed like a couple of years to Bert. Finally, just when he couldn't wait another second, the door swung open and Dad entered. "OK, sport, you guys can be on your own for a few hours today, on two conditions."

"Sure, Dad, anything."

He continued, "First, Emma and Derek are going with you."

Bert was so devastated that he barely heard the rest of what his dad said. Something about cellphones?

"Uh, what, Dad?"

"I said you will keep your cell phone on so that we can contact you if we need to."

Ever since Emma had showed him how to use his cell phone as an EVP recorder, Bert hardly ever had it turned on to receive messages from live people. Ghost hunters use Electronic Voice Phenomenon recorders to record messages from the other side. Bert had a collection of sounds he had accumulated that anyone with a healthy imagination could interpret as words.

The foursome were instructed to meet the adults in front of the cupola of the seminary at four o'clock sharp.

The parents dropped them off at the Meredith Avenue rest area on the Chambersburg Pike with many admonishments, among them to make sure to use enough sunblock and to use the restrooms, not the trees. This last was pointedly directed at Derek by his mother.

"OK, Mom," said Derek with an impish smile. But when he heard Emma's giggle, his ears turned bright red.

"It's a guy thing," muttered Bert low enough that no one but Derek heard.

"Mom, how could you?" said Ronnie, her cheeks gaining splotchy red highlights.

As the parents departed for a day of antiquing, Bert saw the look on his father's face and knew he'd rather spend the day biking with the kids than window shopping.

"Let's go, guys," Bert called, swinging his leg over the seat of his bike and pedaling out of the parking lot.

The little group set out southward, then turned east on Meredith Avenue until they got to Reynolds, just a few hundred feet away. It was easy pedaling on the paved roads that criss-crossed the slightly rolling farmland that had become a battlefield.

Bert turned left and headed north on Reynolds Avenue in the direction the tour arrow pointed.

"Why are we turning away from town?" asked Ronnie.

Emma piped up, "Because the battle started to the north. This way we can follow the battle in the order it took place."

"Yeah," said Bert. "Something like that." And the little troop fell in behind him.

Hey, he thought, *this leading stuff isn't so bad.*

The four rode north past the Railroad Cut, where a thousand Confederate soldiers were captured during the first day of the battle. Then they rode to the Eternal Light

Peace Memorial, parked their bikes next to the roadside, and walked up to the imposing column with the burning fire on top.

Ronnie stood before the brass plaque and read, "Eternal Light Peace Memorial. Dedicated by President Franklin D. Roosevelt during the observance of the 75th anniversary of the Battle of Gettysburg. July 3, 1938."

Walking around the memorial, Bert called out, "Here's another one. It says, 'Peace Eternal in a Nation United.' Well, at least we never went to war against ourselves again after the Civil War."

As they walked back to their bikes, Bert asked Emma,

"What does your little magic box say about this memorial?"

"It's not magic, Bert. It's just an iPhone."

The group of four gathered around their bikes and, sipped from their water bottles as Emma read from her iPhone: "The Eternal Light Peace Memorial was dedicated --"

"Yeah, we know all that. We just read it on the memorial itself. What else does it say?" asked Derek.

"OK, wait a minute," said Emma, scanning the screen. "It was placed on the battlefield on the 75th anniversary of the battle in the presence of 1,800 Civil War veterans and a quarter of a million people. Nearly 100,000 more people were stuck in the giant traffic jams around Gettysburg and never saw the dedication or heard the president speak."

"Here's some more," she continued. "Although there are yearly remembrances and reunions at the battlefield and the site of Lincoln's address of November 19, this was the last official reunion of veterans of the battle."

"Oh, and here's more," she went on, but the boys were already pedaling away.

"I think that's enough," Ronnie said, patting her on the shoulder in a sisterly way. "You don't want to cram too much information into a guy's head. They just can't absorb it."

The two girls got on their bikes and followed the boys, who seemed to be racing.

Emma laughed, gave her head a shake, and said, "Boys!"

Ronnie smiled and kept pace as they closed in on their brothers.

Out of breath and laughing, all four dropped their bikes on the grass near the intersection of Chambersburg Pike and Reynolds Avenue.

"Look," said Bert. "Isn't that the monument to those guys from Pennsylvania that Mom was talking about yesterday?"

"Yeah," replied Derek. "Can you imagine what they felt with a zillion rebels trying to kill them?"

"It'd be great to be able to talk to one of them," said Bert, walking to the front of the memorial and running his hand over the carving of Sergeant Crippen.

"Well, you can read the letters they wrote home," contributed Emma. "My iPhone says that that's how historians reconstructed the soldiers lives."

"No, Emma. You don't understand. I mean that I'd like to be able to actually talk to one of them for real."

"Yeah, like that's gonna happen," said Emma.

Ronnie set her water bottle down and interrupted, "Maybe there is a way. Emma, have you ever heard of a séance?"

Emma replaced her tablet computer in its carry bag and said disdainfully, "Of course. It's when people think they're talking to ghosts. But everybody knows there's no such thing as ghosts. Outside of books, that is."

Bert lit up. He asked Ronnie, "What do you know about séances?"

"Just what I've read," she admitted. "And the conditions here are all wrong. It's nowhere near midnight, the sun is shining bright, and we don't have a medium to channel the spirits."

She continued, "But from what your mother said about all the people who got killed here, some of the spirits might still be hanging around."

"Right," Bert said. "Mom told me Gettysburg is one of the most haunted places in America."

Emma cut in, "There's no such thing as ghosts."

Derek said, "Kew-el. Let's find some."

After some more discussion, they decided to try a little séance of their own right there on the battlefield. They picked out a spot behind the memorial to the Pennsylvania 143rd volunteers and sat in a circle holding hands.

"I feel stupid. What if somebody sees us?" asked Emma.

"I mean, trying to talk to ghosts and all."

"How do you think I feel sitting here holding hands with girls?" replied Derek with a shudder.

"OK, OK, let's just do it," said Bert.

Ronnie said, "Now everybody close your eyes and think real hard about all the soldiers who died on this battlefield."

Deepening her voice, she intoned, "Spirits of Gettysburg, hear me. If you are here, make yourselves known."

Just then the sun passed behind a cloud and the group briefly felt an icy breath.

Bert took this as a sign. He squeezed Emma's and Ronnie's hands tighter while he concentrated on the ghosts of Gettysburg.

Emma gave a little yelp, "Stop it Bert. You're hurting me."

Ronnie shushed her and went on, "We are here to talk with you and gain knowledge from your experiences in this hallowed place."

"Now I really feel stupid," said Derek. "Besides, someone's coming."

They broke the circle and stood up, brushing the dust from their jeans.

"Oh, well," Ronnie said. "It was worth a try."

"I knew it wouldn't work," said Emma. They all walked around to the front of the memorial again.

A kid dressed as a Union drummer was standing in front of the monument tracing the carving with his fingertips.

The drummer looked up at the four and said, "You know, he actually died over there a ways. They put the monument closer to the road so people could see it easier."

"Who are you? And what are you dressed up for, a reenactment or something?" Emma asked.

"Kew-el," said Derek.

CHAPTER 5

THE GHOST

The little soldier took off his kepi, revealing a mass of unruly blonde hair, and said, "My name is Abner Russell and I am a drummer for Company E of the Pennsylvania 143rd Volunteers. I am not dressed up for anything. This is my uniform."

"How do you know where Sergeant Crippen died?" Ronnie asked.

Abner looked from Emma to Ronnie and said, "I know where Sergeant Ben died because I watched him fall."

Bert asked, "Where did you come from? I didn't see you here before."

Turning his attention to Bert, the boy said, "I was here before. I come from a little town you've probably never heard of up north."

"Nice costume, but how did you get here?" inquired Derek.

The drummer answered, "You called me here."

Bert rolled his eyes skyward and thought, *O-M-G. Just great. We're stuck out in the middle of this field with a looneytoon.*

Before anyone had a chance to react, the drummer boy continued, "And, I need your help."

Derek, arms akimbo, announced to the world at large, "Wait a minute. You say your name is Abner, but you don't look like any boy I know. You look like a girl to me."

The drummer twisted the dark blue kepi between small hands and said, "I've kept my secret for so long, I guess it's about time to come clean."

Bert said, "Look kid. If you're lost, maybe we can help you find your folks." He looked around, but the only vehicles in the area were their bikes.

Wiping a tear on the cuff of her uniform, the drummer continued, "My real name is Abigail Russell. I took my brother Abner's place when he got hurt on the farm. I'm big for my age, and his uniform fit me."

Derek said, "So I'm right. You are a girl!"

Abigail nodded and said, "How could you tell? Even after a couple of months, nobody in Company E knew."

Derek replied, "I never saw a boy with a face as pretty as yours." His ears glowed red, offsetting the whiteness of his hair.

Emma punched him in the arm and said, "Boys!"

Abigail smiled and said, "They never change."

Emma asked, "What kind of help do you need?"

That was when things got complicated. Ronnie picked out a spot behind the monument that offered a some shade and the five kids sat on the grass behind the monument to eat their lunched. They offered Abigail some, but she said she wasn't hungry. While the others ate, Abigail told them her story.

She left out nothing, starting when she mustered in with the 143rd Pennsylvanians to take her injured brother's place and ending with her body being wrapped in the nice officer's gray greatcoat.

"It didn't make me feel any warmer, but for some reason, it made me feel just a little better."

Her story ended at the same time as their lunches. They all gathered up anything that fell on the grass to put in the proper receptacle later. Ronnie took everybody's bread crusts and leftover pieces of cookies and scattered them near a bush for the birds.

Bert wiggled his head side to side to work out any kinks, looked at Abigail, and said, "You really are a ghost?"

Abigail nodded.

Emma said, "Prove it."

Abigail said, "Watch."

She disappeared into the granite monument. Seconds later, she came back through.

"Whoa!" cried Bert, jumping back a bit.

Emma walked toward Abigail with her right arm extended. It passed clean through Abigail's shoulder.

Abigail giggled. "That tickles."

"Your shoulder feels like ice water," Emma accused.

"Well, what did you expect? After all, I'm dead," Abigail said.

Ronnie stood awestruck. She had finally met a ghost.

"Kew-el," said Derek.

As Abigail stepped back through the monument, she said, "Now do you believe me?"

Speechless, Emma nodded. Ronnie and Bert were also dumbstruck, but accepted Abigail's ghostliness more easily than Emma.

Derek was never speechless. He asked, "How did you go to the bathroom with all those guys around all the time?"

Abigail blushed. Actually her pale complexion turned a little dusty which is as close to a blush as a ghost can get.

"What kind of help could you possibly need?" Derek asked. "You can live forever."

"No Derek," she replied. "It's not like being alive. I spend long, long periods just lying in my grave until something calls me out of it.

"Sometimes it's because a relative of mine is visiting the battlefield. Sometimes it's because another long-dead soldier wants to talk to me. Once in a while, it's because someone calls me from my grave like you did."

"You mean that just because we all held hands and called you, you came out?" Ronnie asked.

"No, it's not that simple. Something has to disturb me in my grave for me to be able to appear like this. Something that involves extreme emotions."

Emma, ever practical, interrupted, "You're getting off the subject. Why do you need our help and what kind of help do you need?"

Bert rolled his eyes and thought, *sometimes Emma could be downright rude.*

"I need help with two things," she said.

She explained that for all these years she had been buried right where the road was being reconstructed at the intersection. She told them that a few days ago she had been dug up and then dumped in a pile of rocks and dirt. When that pile was used to fill in the hole, her body would be back in the ground, under a paved road again, and it might be another 150 years before she would be able to ask for help again.

"But what can we do to help?" Ronnie asked, hoping the new group visiting the monument couldn't overhear her.

"I can't really rest and join all my family and friends who have passed on until my body is located and identified as a Union soldier. The way I'm buried, wrapped up in that nice man's coat, makes people think I was a rebel. Until that gets straightened out, I must remain here at the battlefield waiting, just waiting, maybe forever.

I need you find my body and give it a proper burial. Then, and only then, can I rest."

She tuned her head to the side. It looked to Bert as if

she was wiping away a tear. *How do we do that?* he thought.

Even Derek was silent for a few moments while what Abigail had just told them sank in.

But he couldn't be silent for long. "That's only one thing. What's the other?" he asked.

An insistent beeping sound cut off her answer. It was Emma's iPhone.

Emma retrieved it from her backpack and yelled, "Bert? Bert! BERRTT!"

"What?" he demanded.

"It's three-forty five," she said. "If we leave now, we can just about make it."

"Omigod! We're supposed to be at the Seminary no later than four o'clock," he sputtered. "Abigail, will you be here tomorrow? If we don't leave right now to meet our parents, we'll get grounded and then we won't be able to help you at all."

"That's right," said Ronnie. "If you meet us here tomorrow, we'll do whatever we can to help you."

"If you're a ghost, why ain't I scared?" wondered Derek.

"You've watched too many horror movies," Emma told him as he ducked to avoid getting smacked in the back of the head.

"Missed me," he crowed.

Abigail ignored Derek and answered Ronnie instead. "I'm always here. All you must do is to hold hands and call, just like you did before."

The others waved good-bye, hopped on their bikes and pedaled furiously toward the Seminary cupola. On the way, they made a pact of secrecy. No grown-ups would learn of the ghost.

"Lets make it a blood oath," said Derek.

"No," Ronnie called back over her shoulder, "Cross your heart and hope to die will do fine."

That evening Bert and Ronnie put their heads together at the evening campfire. "What do you think we can do to help Abigail?" he asked.

"I'm not sure," whispered Ronnie. "I just know that we need to do whatever we can."

"I never met anyone like her before," mused Bert. "You know, she actually *died* fighting for what was right. I don't know if I could ever do that."

Ronnie turned toward Bert and smiled. "Bert, I think you'd be surprised what you can do. But I wouldn't. I know that you have what it takes inside you."

Bert blushed and changed the subject. "You know, she seems kind of nice. Not at all like the ghosts I've read about."

"Well, of course she's nice," replied Ronnie. "She's just a kid like us, only dead."

"Uhh, Ronnie? That's a pretty big difference."

Emma was showing Derek all the apps she had put on her iPhone to use in their quest to help Abigail.

"Now, with this app, the iPhone can become a digital voice recorder so that we can pick up EVPs."

"Kew-el. What's an EVP?"

"It means Electronic Voice Phenomenon. That's how ghosts talk. It can be picked up only with a digital recorder."

"If you can't hear them without one of those thingies, maybe they aren't talking to you."

"Whatever," said Emma, exasperated. But she

continued, "Now this app makes the phone into a EMF meter to detect ghosts' electromechanical field. That way, you can tell when they're near you."

The group around the campfire raised a raucous rendition of, "Great green gobs of greasy, grimy gopher guts," interrupting her explanation. Derek immediately joined in, followed shortly by Emma and the two of them wound up on the ground in fits of laughter.

When everything settled down again, a round of not-too-hot chocolate and cookies with mushy marshmallowy centers disappeared in the campers' mouths. Then the fire was put out and they went to bed.

Bert had a hard time falling asleep. He had never made an appointment with a ghost before. And Ronnie thought he had what it took to be brave.

CHAPTER 6

I CAN'T REST

Bert rubbed the sleep from his eyes and woke up to Emma begging their mother.

"But Mom, we promised!" she wheedled.

"I'm sorry, honey," Mom answered, "But you should know better than to make plans without consulting Dad or me. Who did you promise?"

"We promised Abigail!" Emma blurted out.

Bert was fully awake now and out of bed, making throat-slashing signs to Emma so she would shut up.

"Who's Abigail?" asked Mom, "and why didn't you tell me about her? You know that I like to hear about all your friends."

Bert edged over to the dinette and helped himself to a cinnamon roll.

"I'm sorry, Mom," he said around a mouthful of roll. "It's my fault. I meant to tell you last night at supper. I just forgot."

"Don't talk with your mouth full. Forgot what?"

He washed down the roll with some orange juice, then licked the stickiness from his fingers. "We met this really cool kid named Abigail. She knows all about the history of Gettysburg and the battle. She said if we meet her today, she'll tell us all about the first day of the battle. You know: who was where, who fought who, and some things that most people don't know."

He paused to take a breath. Mom interrupted, "Who fought whom."

"Right, Mom. Anyway, we promised to meet her again today because she made it sound so interesting. For instance, did you know that General Reynolds didn't even get a chance to place his men where he wanted before he was shot off his horse?"

"Bert, you know you should've asked before making a promise like that," she said, already relenting. "Dad and I planned on taking a little drive over to York to tour the Harley-Davidson plant. I thought you'd like it too."

Bert had an idea. "What if you and Dad do that, and

Emma and I go to the battlefield? You won't even need to give us a ride. It's only a couple of miles from here. And it's only a two-lane road, not a super highway or something. I promise that we'll ride out of the way of cars and be real, real careful, stopping at crossings and all. We could be back here by supper time. Please?"

"Let me talk to Dad."

"OK," answered Bert, brightening. When Mom said she was going to talk to Dad, that was almost as good as a yes.

A knock on the door broke into their discussion – which in Bert's opinion wasn't a bad thing. It was Ronnie and Derek's mom.

"Shannon," she called, "It looks as if we have a small insurrection on our hands. The kids seem to prefer their own company to ours. What do you think?"

"Hmmm," said Bert's mom, "I don't know. It sounds like me when I was their age." She laughed. "Is that a good thing?"

Bert's dad could be heard from outside, "Josh and I have no objection, if you and Heather think it's OK."

"OK with me, just so long as they keep in touch."

Shortly thereafter the parents headed east on Route 30, followed by the kids on their bikes.

"Whew, that was a close one," said Bert, puffing a bit to keep up with Derek and Ronnie. "For a minute I thought Emma was gonna spill the beans. But she came through like a champ when push came to shove."

"Hey, big brother," Emma called out. "I know how to keep a secret or two."

As she sped past Bert, she gave him her best smile.

For a second, distrust bit at him. Then he banished it

and smiled back. Life was good.

"You know what?" said Derek, weaving from side to side in front of Bert. "Your parents are kew-el."

Bert had never thought of his parents that way. Remembering that he was supposed to be the leader of the troop, he yelled, "Gangway! Coming through!" He took his place at the front of the pack.

Other people were already at the memorial when they arrived.

A nice lady with curly gray hair and glasses perched so far toward the tip of her nose that Bert wondered why they didn't fall off read to a little boy from her guidebook. "Now you must watch your manners here, Joshua. Be respectful. On this very spot, a man from Pennsylvania was killed in battle."

Standing a short distance away, Bert refrained from correcting her. He noticed that Emma looked ready to burst from the effort of keeping her mouth shut.

Derek hopped from leg to leg, holding two fingers up behind Emma's head. When Emma noticed him, she grabbed his hand and forced it behind his back while twisting the offending fingers. This resulted in yelps from Derek. The lady left in a huff muttering something about rowdy teenagers.

Derek said, "Kew-el. She thinks we're teenagers."

Bert almost felt like apologizing, but felt it wasn't his fault.

The gray-haired lady and the little kid had barely gotten to their car when Emma grabbed Bert's hand and, dragged him around behind the memorial. "Come on. Let's call Abigail."

They sat on the ground holding hands. Ronnie called

out, "Abigail? Abigail? Where are you? It's us. We're back."

Abigail walked out of the memorial and said, "You don't have to yell. I'm dead, not deaf. I'm right here."

"I wish you wouldn't do that," said Bert.

"Sorry," said Abigail, but her smile showed she wasn't.

Derek said, "How come I can't see through you?"

Abigail kept smiling. "Because I don't want you to."

Bert asked, "What kind of help do you need?"

As soon as Abigail started to reply, another car pulled up. A group of adults got out and fawned all over the memorial. After they were interrupted three times in a row, Abigail suggested they meet at the cannons along the edge of the woods, a mile or so away.

"OK," said Derek. "We'll race you."

"You'll lose," answered Abigail. She was gone in a "pouff."

"I wish she wouldn't do that," Bert sighed.

Derek was the first biker to the line of cannons. Abigail was waiting for him. She waved him over to a gun emplacement where wheeled cannon rested under the canopy of trees along Confederate Avenue.

"OK, how did you do it?" he demanded.

She smiled and said, "It's a ghost thing. You wouldn't understand."

Emma placed her hand on the long barrel of the cannon and said, "Oh, wow. A Napoleon!"

Derek said, "I thought Napoleon was one of those dead French guys."

Abigail smiled tolerantly and said, "Derek, Napoleon is the name of this cannon. It could shoot a 12-pound cannonball nearly a mile."

"Why was it called a Napoleon?" Derek wondered.

"I don't know," came the answer. "I'm just a drummer."

With just a touch of smugness, Emma reported, "The gun was originally called the emperor of cannons. Since Napoleon was the Emperor of France, they called it the Napoleon. I looked it up with my iPhone."

"I'll bet Mom knows without even looking it up," She added. "She knows a lot about everything."

Yeah, thought Bert, *as long as it happened a zillion years ago.*

The little group pushed their bikes into the woods and sat in the shade.

"So you're a drummer, right?" asked Derek.

"That's right," Abigail answered.

"What's a drummer do that's so important? Why would an army need music?" he asked.

Abigail directed her attention to Derek, but she included everyone in her answer. "You know that war is a pretty noisy thing."

They all nodded.

"As a matter of fact," she continued, "it gets so noisy that nobody can hear anybody else, even when they yell. That's where we come in. Our drums and bugles can be heard over the noise of battle. We stand near the officers and they tell us what signals to send to the soldiers. Different bugle calls and different drum cadences mean different things."

"Like what?" Derek asked.

"For instance, everybody knows what the bugle call 'Charge' sounds like. Maybe the commander wants the enemy to think one thing while our men do something else."

"So?"

"So he gives me an order to beat a drum cadence that changes the meaning of the next bugle call. Then, when the bugler calls 'charge,' our men do something else, and the enemy is fooled."

"Where's your gun?"

"Buglers and drummers don't have guns."

"You mean you go into battle, guns shooting and explosions going off all around you, and you don't even carry a gun?"

"That's right."

Derek squinched up his face, thinking hard. Then he brightened, nodded, and said, "You guys are the bravest of the brave. I'll do whatever I can to help you."

"He must really like her," Emma muttered to no one in particular.

Abigail looked from Emma to Derek and just smiled.

Then Ronnie said, "Yesterday Abigail you said there were two things you need us to do. What's the other one?"

Abigail paced to and fro for a bit before answering. "First of all, you know I'm dead, right?"

"If you say so," commented Bert. "But you look pretty alive to me."

"Yeah, how do we know you aren't just tricking us?" Emma demanded.

"I think you're just too pretty to be a ghost," said Derek.

Ronnie said nothing.

"I look like this to you so that you won't get upset.

Would you like to see how I really look?" She shifted her drum sticks from her belt to a pocket on her britches. Then she turned a full circle. When she faced them again, she was a maggoty mess with dirt dribbling from her vacant eye sockets and her teeth poking through scraps of skin that clung to her skull. Her uniform was riddled with tears and holes and one of her legs was completely missing.

"Eee-yowl!" screamed Emma. Before anyone else had a chance to move, she was a hundred feet away, pedaling furiously for anywhere else.

Ronnie sat down on the grass, open-mouthed, wide-eyed and pale. Bert gulped and gulped to keep his breakfast where it belonged. For some reason, he couldn't move.

Derek's eyes brightened and his face split in a grin. "Kew-el. Can you show me how to do that?"

Abigail didn't hear him because she had already disappeared and reappeared in her more familiar form in front of Emma's speeding bike.

Emma slid her bike to a sideways stop to avoid hitting Abigail who called out, "Emma, I'm truly sorry. I didn't mean to scare you. But you were all acting like I was joking around. I had to show you."

Abigail floated alongside Emma as they returned to the group at the cannon line.

Once there, she explained that ghosts can appear either the way they were just before they died or the way their body is now. Everyone agreed that they liked her better just the way she was. She promised to never again appear to them in the other way.

While Abigail told the story of how she wound up

stuck at the battleground, the others sat on and around the artillery piece listening attentively. Even Derek paid close attention.

When she got to the part where the man from cemetery registration threw her body back into the ditch, they all uttered sounds of disgust.

"Don't be angry with him," she said. "Feelings were running pretty high around then. I imagine the Confederate people did pretty much the same to Billy Yank."

"Billy Yank?" said Derek. "Who's that?"

Abigail explained, "We called them Johnny Reb and they called us Billy Yank. It was just the way we were."

Ronnie tilted her head to one side, "OK, that's pretty much explains *how* you got here. But why can't you *leave*?"

"It has to do with family honor," she said. "You see, my body was never identified and given a proper burial. I posed as my brother Abner, so he is officially listed as missing in action. To a lot of folk that's as good as saying I deserted. I wouldn't leave this battlefield, if I could."

The drummer girl rubbed her right eye with a knuckle and continued, "Until my body gets dug up and recognized as that of a Union soldier, I can't rest. I can't join my mummy and poppy and my brothers and sisters, even though they passed over so many years ago."

Bert got up and put his arm around her shoulder, not even noticing her ghostliness. He said, "We'll do whatever it takes to help you get back with your family."

Emma asked, "OK, what do we need to do?"

Abigail replied, "Just get me dug up and reburied as a Union soldier."

"Don't sound like no prob to me," Derek said while trying to swallow soda at the same time. Somehow he didn't seem very reassuring with soda dribbling down his chin.

"Doesn't sound like any problem," corrected Emma.

"Who died and left you English teacher?" Derek wanted to know.

"Shut up or I'll make you eat dirt!" replied Emma.

"Knock it off, you two!" yelled Bert. In a quieter tone, he told Abigail, "It sounds like a no-brainer to me. We'll fix you up I a jiffy."

Ronnie said, "Let's say we can figure a way to get you reburied. What's the other thing you need help with?"

"Remember you wanted to know about the other thing that I needed help with?"

"Well,"I'm not quite alone," Abigail replied.

CHAPTER 7

JESSE IS DEAD TOO

"What?" all four demanded at once.

"I have a friend."

They just stared at her.

"Jesse," she explained.

"Who's Jesse?" Ronnie asked.

"It's sort of complicated," Abigail replied.

"The sooner you tell us, the sooner we can do

something about it," said Bert.

Abigail told them the story of the Confederate soldier whose greatcoat she was buried in. When he died, his brother said that he'd take the coat back to Jesse's mom. But instead he wrapped Abigail's body in it. Now, Jesse's essence was stuck at the Gettysburg battlefield as well until he got his coat back.

"Well," said Emma. "Where is this Jesse?"

"You've got to call him, just like you did me. But, before you do, I must warn you that Jesse has a bit of an attitude problem. Sometimes he likes to scare people."

"That's simple. We just won't call him," said Ronnie.

"No, wait," said Abigail. "let me go talk to him."

She was back in a matter of seconds. "Jesse promised not to scare you," she said.

The four then held hands and said, "Jesse. We are calling you. If you are here, please make yourself known."

A wisp of smoke started dribbling from the mouth of the cannon. Where it hit the ground, a young soldier took form from the feet up. When his head was in view, he solidified and stepped forward. They saw a barefoot young man who was as skinny as a string bean. He carried a large-bore rifle across his shoulders.

"Private Jesse Coltrane of the Confederate States of America Army of Northern Virginia," he said with a pleasing Southern twang."I would say that I am at your service, except that I assume you are members of the Army of Oppression that has invaded my homeland. No offense, but when it comes to accepting help, I don't think I need yours."

Abigail interrupted him, stamping her foot on the

ground, which of course made no sound whatever. "Jesse Samuel Coltrane, now you just stop it. The war is over. Regardless how you feel, you're just going to have accept help from us Yankees so that we can both get on with our afterlives."

She turned to the others and explained, "Sometimes he forgets the war is over."

Jesse said, "I'd do anything to get my coat back from this thieving little Yankee." But he softened his words with a winsome smile and put his arm around Abigail's shoulders. It was obvious that he felt protective towards her.

Then he noticed Ronnie. Walking over to her, he looked her up and down, then said, "Well, if you aren't the prettiest little Yankee I've seen in a couple of lifetimes. What's your name?"

Bert shouldered his way between them and said, "Ronnie. What's it to you?"

Jesse laughed and said, "Ronnie? I didn't ask for your name, boy."

Bert didn't know why he felt so hot all of a sudden.

Ronnie pushed Bert out of the way and said with a smile, "Why, thank you for the nice words Private Coltrane. My name is Veronica, but my friends call me Ronnie."

Bert walked over to the bikes, hands jammed deep in his pockets. He kicked a cinder out into the road.

While Jesse was entertaining Ronnie, Derek, and Emma, Abigail whispered in Bert's ear, "It doesn't mean anything. That's the way Jesse talks all the time. Besides, I think you're cuter than he is. And so does Ronnie."

Bert looked up with a start, but Abigail was already

back with the group. When he rejoined them, he heard Jesse say, "Go on, Abigail. Tell 'em where you are. And tell 'em what that Yankee bull-dozer driver did to you."

Eyes downcast, Abigail told them about the dozer driver finding her. "Then he scooped me up and dumped me into one of those big trucks."

The kids stared at her aghast. Emma said, "That's awful! Why would they do that?"

"Something about getting the job done on time and making more money," responded Abigail. She continued, "The truck took me for a little ride and dumped me in a big pile of dirt and rocks that they are going to use to fill in a ditch."

Silence descended while Abigail's statements were digested.

Bert had an idea. "Abigail, can you show us where you were originally buried?"

She explained that her so-called grave was under Seminary Avenue, not far from the seminary itself. The site of her grave was about to be paved over as part of the road reconstruction project.

"What are we waiting for?" called Bert as he stuffed his soda back into his backpack and headed for his bike. "Let's go."

"Where?" called Emma back.

"To the seminary," Bert tossed back over his shoulder. "Once we get there, Abigail can show us the exact location."

The bikes skidded a bit on the cinders at the edge of Confederate Avenue, raising some dust. Then they caught traction and sped off.

A while later they were in the pre-anniversary throng

around the seminary. They looked for Abigail.

Derek saw the drummer facing away in the crowd. He ran up to her and placed his hand on her shoulder. "Abigail! Here we are."

A rather upset young man in full Union uniform turned around and said, "Who are you calling Abigail?" He gave Derek a push in the chest.

Derek lowered his head, clenched his fists, and made ready to charge, but Ronnie grabbed him by the back of his T-shirt and said, "Sorry. Our mistake. No harm done."

Emma looked at Derek with something between admiration and revulsion and asked, "Would you really fight that older kid? He would have taken you apart."

"Nobody pushes me and gets away with it," replied Derek. "He might have won, but he'd know that he'd fought a Griffin."

"Kew-ell," replied Emma.

Abigail showed up and interrupted them. "Come on, it's just a little ways from here."

"Lead on," said Bert. The little troop followed Abigail northward on Seminary Avenue to where it intersected Route 30.

Pointing to a spot about two feet out from the curb, she said, "There it is, the spot where I lay for nearly 150 years. I was about five feet down."

Bumper-to-bumper traffic crawled along, missing the spot only because orange traffic cones festooned with blinkers and flags separated the construction area from the main highway.

Abigail pointed to a surface scraped clean of paving. Flattened clay and shale were exposed about a foot or so below the pavement level.

They clambered down to the spot she indicated.

Bert said, "You mean you were under the road?"

"Uh-huh," said Abigail. "You're standing on my grave right now."

They all jumped back from where they were standing and Abigail laughed. "I'm not there anymore."

Bert got down on all fours and began frantically scrabbling at the spot with his hands. "Geez, I could really use a shovel right now," he commented.

"Bert, what are you doing?" asked Ronnie. "She just said she's not there anymore."

"But if we can find something Abigail was wearing or carrying, I'll bet they'll need to stop working until everything gets straightened out."

The other three joined him in trying to unearth some evidence of Abigail's burial.

Abigail looked on hopefully. Jesse commented, "Crazy Yankees."

Bert worked at an irregular flat piece of rock about four inches in diameter.

"Maybe I can work this one loose," he said.

He reached in his pocket and came out with a quarter, which he used as around the edge of the rock. When he finally worked the rock loose, he flipped it over. Stuck to the dirt on the bottom of the rock was a small metal tube with a couple of rings at the top and a couple of rings at the bottom. It was about two inches long.

"Look what I found," Bert said. The other three grouped around him to see.

"It's one of my drum stick carriages," Abigail explained.

The others looked at her quizzically.

"A drum stick carriage is a a metal tube that fits on the drum sling. It's a place to put drum sticks when you aren't using them or to hold your spares."

Right then, a big man wearing a white hard hat, a grimy T-shirt with the sleeves cut off, and brown work pants clumped over to them. "What're you kids doing there?" He yelled. "Get out of there right now!"

Bert tried to reason with him. "Mister, you've got to stop digging. Look what we found." Bert handed him the metal artifact.

The man held it up to the light and turned it first this way, then that way. He then reached back, winding up, and threw it for all he was worth.

"It's just a piece of junk that fell off one of the tractors. Now get out of here before I call the police." His voice rising until it could be heard over all the sounds of construction.

He turned on his heel and clumped toward a bunch of highway workers who were giving pointers to a crew member on how to twirl the "Stop-Slow" sign she was using to control the traffic flow. She was the only one in the crew actually working.

"Houston, we have a problem," said Emma.

"Who's Houston?" asked Abigail

"It's a figure of speech," explained Ronnie. "What Emma means is that digging you up isn't going to be as simple as just digging you up."

"Hunh?" said Derek.

"Let's go where we can think," said Bert. They climbed back onto the sidewalk and biked to a place where they could talk undisturbed. It was under a big sycamore tree that stood alongside a quiet, cool brook at the edge of the battlefield not too far from where they had started their day at the Pennsylvania 143rd monument.

"See this little stream?" asked Abigail. "It's called Willoughby Run. Seemed like thousands of Confederate soldiers came out of here and up McPherson Ridge at us on that day."

"My big brother was one of them," Jesse said, puffing up his chest.

"All this bike riding is making me hungry," said Derek. He reached into his knapsack and withdrew a wrapped sandwich.

In short order, they were all sitting on a log that spanned the creek dangling their bare feet in the cool water. The kids who were alive were eating sandwiches and drinking soda.

They spent the rest of the afternoon making and discarding plans. Finally, they decided that a night operation was in order.

CHAPTER 8

BUSTED!

It was that time between midnight and sunrise when anything can happen, and usually does.

"Bert?" whispered Ronnie. "Did you get everything?"

"I found an old army trenching tool that Dad keeps in the motor home, a couple of bottles of water and some cookies. What did you bring?"

Still whispering as they pushed their bikes through the grass on the way to the main road, she replied, "I got a couple of Mom's big serving spoons and some cold soda."

Derek piped up, "Don't forget me. I took the stakes from the horseshoe pits. We can use them to break up the ground."

"Compacted clay and shale will be very difficult to break through with just hand tools," opined Emma.

An owl hooted in a nearby tree and Bert nearly jumped out of his skin.

Emma laughed and said, "What are you afraid of, ghosts?"

Everyone, including Bert, laughed, remembering who they were on their way to meet.

Because they had to bike off the road every time a car approached, it took longer to arrive at the Pennsylvania 143rd memorial than during the day.

They stood in a circle behind the stone and called, "Abigail? Abigail? We're here."

"So am I," said a spooky voice behind Bert.

He jumped, turned around, and said, "I really wish you wouldn't do that!"

She giggled and said, "Sorry," though of course she wasn't. Then she said, "Meet you at my old grave" and disappeared.

Ten minutes later they arrived at the intersection of Seminary Avenue and Route 30. She was already there, waiting for them.

"Can you show me how to travel like you?" asked Derek.

"Yes," said Abigail.

"Kew-el!"

"But you have to die first," she continued.

He didn't seem fazed.

All five gathered around the spot.

"Let's start breaking some of these stones with Derek's horseshoe stakes," said Emma. "We can use one of those concrete blocks as a hammer."

"Yeah," said Ronnie, "Then we could pry up the stones with the other stake."

"And then I'll clear away the dirt and smaller stones with the trenching tool," said Bert.

"Someone's coming!" said Abigail. Everybody flattened themselves to the ground except Abigail, who simply disappeared.

Headlights splashed over the construction area as a car made the turn onto Seminary Ridge Avenue and drove away.

Bert lifted his head and watched until the taillights of the car winked out in the distance before whispering, "All clear."

They held hands again and said, "OK, Abigail. You can come back now."

When she returned from wherever ghosts go when they disappear, Derek commented, "You know, for a ghost, you're a real scaredycat."

So many cars, trucks, and delivery vans came past in the next hour that they removed only one large flat piece of shale. They were a mere six inches closer to their goal.

For what seemed like the thousandth time, Abigail called out, "Someone's coming."

This time they kept right on digging. They just

crouched on their knees to lessen the chance of being seen from the road.

Suddenly they were bathed in the beam of light from a powerful flashlight while a voice boomed, "Now what have we here?"

Shielding their eyes from the blinding light, they saw the outline of a large figure wearing a police officer's hat. They all lost the power of speech and froze in place with terror.

They also heard the crackle and spit of a walkie-talkie. They couldn't understand a word, but the police officer did.

He spoke into it. "It's just some kids. I won't need back-up. They'll be my 10-15s and I'll 10-19. I'll be 10-10. 10-4."

He walked them to his SUV. They stowed their bikes and backpacks in the storage space in the back.

"Now, if you desperadoes promise to behave, you can sit in the back seat. Otherwise, I'll have to cuff you."

They promised to behave. Bert, Ronnie, and Emma, all shaking like leaves in a hurricane, got into the back seat which was separated from the front seat by a cage-like screen. Derek had to sit up front front because there were only three seat belts in the back.

The police officer spoke into a microphone. "Unit 151 is 10-8 and will 10-19 with four juvenile 10-15s. Mileage 72,655."

Bert sat glumly in the back seat. He had never even dreamed about being in this much trouble in his life. Under arrest! It made him feel even worse that he had talked Emma into coming along. Well, he'd just tell Mom and Dad that it was all his idea.

Derek was the first one to recover. His curiosity overcame his fear and he asked, as though he hadn't a care in the world, "Mister, what was all that ten talk you were doing?"

The police officer replied, "Call me Officer Hanlon. That ten talk, as you put it, is a kind of radio shorthand . 10-4 means OK, I understand. 10-19 means return to station. 10-10 means out of service but listening to the radio. And, 10-8 means back in service."

"kew-el," said Derek.

Ronnie leaned forward and timidly asked, "Officer Hanlon, what does 10-15 mean?"

"Prisoner in custody."

Silence descended on the four 10-15s in the SUV.

Once they got to the police station, Officer Hanlon put them in a room that smelled like old gym socks. It was painted a dismal green and had a long table in the middle. Some uncomfortable wooden chairs were around the table.

Officer Hanlon sat on one side of the table and directed them to sit on the other side. He opened a notebook and said, "Now, then. Let's get started. What are your names? Where are you from? How can I reach your parents? And last but not least, why in the world were you guys digging at the construction site in the middle of the night?"

They gave him all the information he asked for, plus a feeble excuse about digging for battlefield artifacts. He wrote it all in his notebook, then left them alone in the room. As soon as he left, the kids got out of the chairs. They were too nervous to sit.

"Are we going to jail?" asked Derek. He sounded

more excited than apprehensive.

"I don't think so," answered Emma. "I think they're going to call our parents."

"I'd rather go to jail," said Bert. After all, he was the oldest and supposedly the most mature.

Ronnie just paced back and forth with moist eyes darting around the room, never settling on any one thing.

Please don't cry, Ronnie, thought Bert. *If you start to cry, I don't know what I'll do.*

"Is the town of Gettysburg part of the battlefield?" Ronnie asked.

Emma replied, "I think so. Bullets and cannon balls hit a lot of the buildings in town, so I guess so. Why?"

"If it is, we can call Abigail."

The four held hands and Bert nervously called out, "Abigail? Are you here?"

She appeared right smack in the middle of the table. It looked as though she was cut in half at the waist and her top half set on the table.

"Does that hurt?" Derek wanted to know.

"Geez, Abigail. I wish you wouldn't do that," said Bert.

"Sorry." She moved so that she was clear of the table and they could see all of her. But she wasn't sorry, of course.

"I just wanted you to know that we are in the biggest trouble of our whole lives," said Ronnie.

"Yeah," agreed Bert. "I'll probably be grounded until I'm ninety."

Emma lifted her chin off her chest a bit in an imitation of a nod.

"I don't know about the rest of these guys," continued

Ronnie, but I made a promise to you and I intend to keep it."

"I'm with Ronnie. What's seventy or eighty years of being grounded compared to being cemented into a road?" Bert gave a poor imitation of a brave smile.

Derek agreed with his usual smile and even Emma nodded that she was in.

While they were talking with Abigail, Officer Hanlon came in.

"Who are you kids talking to?" he asked.

They jumped and turned around guiltily.

"No-nobody," said Bert.

"Each other," said Ronnie.

The big police officer looked at them for a few seconds. Then he shook his head and said, "We reached your parents on their cell phones at the campground. They're on their way."

He left, closing the door behind him.

Derek turned back to Abigail. "Why didn't he see you?"

Abigail responded, "Two reasons. One, he didn't call me. Two, I didn't want him to."

Derek wasn't put off that easily. "Why didn't you disappear like you did all those other times someone came?"

"I disappear when I get scared or nervous and can't concentrate. But Office Hanlon is a nice man. He doesn't scare me."

"How about that," said Derek. "A ghost who's scared of people."

CHAPTER 9

THE GAME IS AFOOT

The next few hours were some of the most unpleasant that Bert had ever spent. They were miserable for a lot of reasons. For one, he had disappointed Mom and Dad.

O-M-G, did they ever make that clear. It took Mom over an hour to list all the ways she was disappointed with Bert, starting with his foray into juvenile delinquency and eventually winding up with the lack of responsibility he had shown toward his little sister.

"Not to mention the fact that you exposed yourself and others to who knows what dangers traipsing around the countryside during the middle of the night."

Bert was genuinely sorry that he had brought trouble to his family.

He was even sorrier that he had failed Abigail. What had started as a fun thing to do had evolved into the most important undertaking of his life. This was no longer just ghost stories. This was for real. If Bert failed to keep his promise to Abigail, she might roam the battlefields of Gettysburg forever. Bert couldn't even begin to think what it would be like to be away from Mom and Dad and even Emma for 150 years. And it looked as if Abigail was going to spend even more years away from her mummy and poppy and all her friends and relatives.

Just because Bert had screwed up. Again.

In the end, Bert was grounded for the rest of the vacation. He wasn't allowed to be out of his parents' voice range even around the campground.

Ronnie and Derek's parents didn't see it quite as harshly. They forbade Ronnie and Derek to associate with Bert but permitted them to hang out with Emma because they felt that *she* was a *good influence.*

"It was nice of Officer Hanlon to let us come home with Mom and Dad, instead of sending us to Juvenile Hall," said Emma as she drew circles in the water her lemonade glass had made on the table.

"I guess so," Bert muttered, looking out the window at the campground. "Look, sis, I'm sorry I got you into trouble," he continued, not looking at her.

"Bert, as near as I can tell, you're the only one who got into trouble. The rest of us skated," she said. "And that's good because we can still try to help Abigail."

He shook his head. "But I'm not even allowed to talk to Ronnie. How can we plan anything?"

"That's easy. I can be your contact with Ronnie and Derek. I'll be like one of General Meade's scouts carrying intelligence dispatches between brigades."

"And Derek can be a spy. He'll like that," said Bert, his mood lightening a tiny bit.

They put their heads together and planned their next campaign to free Abigail. And it wasn't even noon.

As Emma scampered out of the camper, her head full of plans, diversions, and some really good ideas of her own, Bert thought that maybe it wasn't so bad having a sister who was a goody-two-shoes. Now he had an undercover partner in the quest to free Abigail!

Bert's dad came into the motor home and walked back toward where Bert was sitting at the dinette. He stopped at the fridge on the way and got a cold can of cola. Bert didn't look up. He felt too sad and embarrassed.

Dan O'Neill sat opposite Bert, popped the can of cola, and took a swig. He said, "Well Magoo, you've really done it this time."

Bert looked up miserably and said, "I'm really sorry, Dad."

"What ever made you do it?"

Bert thought that maybe, just maybe, Dad might understand. So he rushed right in. "Well, there's this little drummer girl who got killed in the battle, except that she was buried in a a rebel's coat. Oh yeah, I forgot to tell you she was Union. And now they're going to pave over her grave and she won't be able to get buried the right way, and she'll never get to be with her mummy and poppy. And--"

"Whoa there, Bert!" his dad said, his forehead wrinkling, eyebrows coming together like the letter V, mouth scrunching up into a look of distaste. "I didn't know you were going to load this up with one of your ghost stories."

Dad raised the cola to his mouth and drank it till there was nothing left. He crushed the can in his hand and lobbed it into the trash can. Then he got up, gave Bert a wistful look and said, "When you're ready to tell me the truth, let me know" The slamming of the screen door provided all the punctuation that the sentence needed.

Bert crossed his arms on the table in front of him then laid his forehead down on them.

*

Just a two-minute walk away, Ronnie Griffin raised her head from the table where she had been resting it. Her parents had lectured her continually since she and Derek rode back to the campground from the police station. She couldn't blame them. This was the worst thing she had ever done.

But - and it was an important thing - she had just about overdosed on "young lady" this and "young lady" that. Mom went so far as to say, "I'd expect something like this from your brother. Boys do things like that."

Boys do things like that? Boys *do things like tha*t?

Since when are boys more adventurous than girls?

She rubbed the errant tear from her eyes on the back of her hand and decided, not for the first time, that anything boys could do, she could do better.

Besides, she had made a promise to reunite Abigail with her family. Even Mom and Dad would agree that it's not honorable to go back on a promise. There just had to be something she could do.

Derek came in and slid into the booth across from her.

"I'm sorry about this mess, sis."

She could hardly believe her ears. Derek never apologized. A character on his fave TV show said that apologizing was a sign of weakness.

"It's OK, Derek. We shouldn't have gone out in the middle of the night like that. Mom and Dad have a right to be angry."

"No, no, no," he replied. "I'm not sorry about going out, I'm sorry about getting caught. We'll just be more careful tonight." Then he gave that patented grin of his guaranteed to get him out of trouble. At least, with Mom.

"Tonight?" she started to say, but a small scratching sound at the window interrupted her. It was Emma.

Before she had a chance to say anything, Emma whispered, "Behind the pool pump house in fifteen minutes."

As one of Ronnie's fave book characters, Sherlock Holmes, liked to say, "The game is afoot."

*

Fifteen minutes later, the three conspirators who

could get away met in the evergreens that screened the pool's pump house from view.

Ten minutes after that, assignments were made and the plan was set in motion.

CHAPTER 10

A BARN DANCE

"Mom, there's a barn dance tonight at the campground's clubhouse. Can I go?"

"On two conditions, young lady: if your brother goes with you, and that O'Neill boy isn't there."

"Bert won't be there, Mom. He's grounded like, forever."

"OK, and don't say like."

"Dad, can I go to the clubhouse after dinner tonight? They're having a square dance. I'd like to learn how to do it. OK?"

"I'll see. Let me talk to Mom."

Yes! Emma turned away smiling. When Dad said, "I'll see," it was almost as good as yes.

*

"Listen, you little twerp. You'd better at least act like you're interested, or this won't work."

"OK Ronnie. I am so, like, into it. Know why they call it as square dance? It's for squares only."

She balled her fists at her side, stood rigidly in place, and stared down at her brother with what he liked to call "the hairy eyeball."

"OK, OK, I'm just kidding. Don't get your underwear in a twist," Derek said, backing up a step.

*

"I'm going to the barn dance tonight and you aren't," Emma said in a singsong voice.

"Don't lay it on too thick," Bert whispered.

*

Dinner was an uncomfortable event in the O'Neill

RV that evening.

Mom and Dad both felt guilty about grounding Bert during vacation, and he wasn't helping any, poking at his food like a condemned prisoner. Emma beamed and showed everyone at the table what her iPhone said about barn dances.

"When the caller says to do-si-do, that means everybody sorta winds in and out around each other."

"Uh-huh," Bert mumbled.

"It'll be fun. Mom and Dad, are you going to come and watch me?"

If Bert's eyes were capable of shooting darts, Emma would be dead.

Mom looked up. "No honey. We're just going to hang around here and decide what to do tomorrow. Maybe we'll take a walk over to the Griffins' and see what they're up to."

Emma shot a knowing glance Bert's way and started clearing the table.

*

The clubhouse at the campground wasn't a house, and neither was it a club. That was OK. The barn dance wasn't taking place in a barn either, and the square dance mostly involved dancing around in circles.

The people who ran the campground did their best with what they had, and what they had was a big picnic pavilion. Most of the picnic benches were moved down to one end and hidden behind a stack of hay bales. Some hay bales were left out for seating. Imitation kerosene lanterns hung from the rafters and colorful bunting was strung up between the posts. What picnic tables remained were covered in gingham checked cloths in either red and white or blue and white. A campground employee oversaw a table laden with soft drinks and snacks.

Opposite the stacked hay bales was a large cleared space for the dancers. Off to one side was an old guy in cowboy clothes holding a microphone in his hand. He introduced himself as Jimmy West, the dance caller.

While they waited for the place to fill up with dancers and would-be dancers, what passed for western music was being played through a couple of large speakers.

All in all, it came across as what it was: a bunch of city folk trying their best to enjoy themselves at an imitation country hoe-down. An atmosphere of forced gaiety greeted Emma, Ronnie, and Derek.

They each got a glass of cowpunchers' punch, which was actually strawberry Kool-Aid, and a giant cow patty, which was what the fake cowgirl giving out the refreshments called a not-too-big chocolate chip cookie.

Emma led them to a picnic table far enough away from the pavilion that the noise wouldn't drown out their conversation. They all sat down at one end and put their heads together. "I made sure my parents won't be here. How about you guys?"

Ronnie said, "I don't know. They may show up later."

Derek said something around a mouthful of cookie and Kool-Aid that sounded like agreement

"Then we'll be quick, OK?"

"How far is it to the battlefield?" asked Derek.

"About three miles," replied Emma.

"If we could run as fast as Olympic athletes, we could

be back in less than a half hour."

"Dream on," said Ronnie.

"We could probably cut a bit off the distance if we go cross-country, but we'd lose that time trying to go through the woods," said Emma.

*

They gave the darkness a bit of time to settle in and then they were off, keeping to the side of the road so they could dart into the bushes when a car appeared. It took them nearly an hour to get to the edge of the battlefield.

Their business took only a couple of minutes and they were heading back to the campground in no time at all. Even though they trotted, jogged, and ran as much as they could, they didn't get back to the barn dance until nearly eleven o'clock.

Out of breath, they entered one side of the pavilion just in time to see all four parents entering the other side.

"Quick," said Emma. She grabbed Ronnie and Derek by their arms and started running around in circles, stamping her feet.

They caught on instantly. In less time than it takes to tell, the three of them were whirling around each other, stamping their feet and making what they thought were cowboy whoops.

Their parents came over to them laughing.

"Hey, guys, we just stopped over to see how you were faring," said Bert and Emma's mom.

"Yeah," said Ronnie and Derek's dad, "Doesn't look like you learned much square dancing, but you sure look like you're having fun."

"How about a little do-si-do?" asked Heather Griffin.

A guilty pall quickly descended on the three dancers but departed just as fast. Sure it was wrong to lie to their parents, but saving Abigail was more important.

They collapsed breathlessly onto a picnic table. Derek pantomimed a man lost in the desert. He embellished his performance, grasping his throat with both hands, while croaking "Water, water, please."

The moms and dads showed their appreciation of the performance by laughing as they sat down.

Ronnie called out to Derek, "While you're getting something to drink don't forget us other thirsty mortals over here."

Emma just looked around with an expression of relief.

Within forty-five minutes everybody was back in their respective RVs, showered and sound asleep. Everybody that is, except the kids. They were feigning sleep.

CHAPTER 11

"FOR ABIGAIL!"

It was one-thirty a.m. on one of those nights when the moon peeks around the edges of the clouds, every so often illuminating a patch of ground with a cold blue light.

One of those nights when you get the shivers even if

you're warm.

Emma and Bert were the first to get to the pump house behind the pool. Ronnie and Derek arrived a few minutes later. The four set out silently on their mission to the battlefield. They were slowed somewhat by their lack of bicycles and the times they had to dive for cover when vehicles passed them on the road.

It took an hour and change to get to the Pennsylvania 143rd Monument on Chambersburg Pike. From that point, they could see that the intersection with Seminary Ridge Avenue was lighted like day.

"Abigail?" Bert called softly. She was suddenly in front of them.

"What's going on?" he asked.

"They're working all night to get done before the anniversary of the battle," she replied.

"Oh, great. Only one day left," Emma said.

"Not quite," said Abigail.

"How's that?" Derek asked.

"They're going to try to pave it over in the morning," she replied.

"That means they'll be using the tailing pile in a few hours," Derek said.

"Uh-huh."

"Then let's get going. Time's a-wasting," said Emma.

"Show us where it is," said Ronnie to Abigail.

"Follow me."

She pouffed out of sight, then reappeared a couple of seconds later. "I'm sorry. I forgot," she said. She began floating along the battlefield toward Seminary Ridge where it intersected with Route 30. Her four corporeal helpers had to walk.

They arrived near the intersection and hid behind some bushes to reconnoiter.

A giant Caterpillar front-loader sat off to one side with its diesel engine burbling while a scruffy-looking guy in a shirt with the sleeves cut off relaxed at the controls.

The rest of the crew were scuttling about the construction site doing their various jobs. One guy was in charge of the two trailers, each of which had four huge floodlights, one at either end of the construction site. The intersection was lighted like noon.

Four other paving machines were lined up in a row at the beginning of the excavation panting like monstrous insects ready for prey. First in line was a tri-axle dump truck with a full load of warm asphalt. Right behind it was a strange-looking thing with treads that had a big hopper box in the front for the tri-axle to dump its load into. Leading up from that hopper was a conveyor belt that took the asphalt up, over, and into the next machine, where it would be heated some more and then deposited on the roadway. Bringing up the rear of the little convoy was a humongous roller that would compress, flatten out, and smooth the asphalt. After that last machine passed through, all that was left to do was to wait while the asphalt cooled. Then the line painters could put down the lane, edge, and intersection markers.

The workers who operated all these machines were standing around drinking coffee, talking, and waiting for the front-loader to back fill the excavation

If they succeeded, Abigail would once again be under the road.

One man ran from machine to machine and crew

member to crew member shouting orders frantically around an unlit cigar. His words could barely be heard over the sound of all the diesel engines idling. "Let's get this show on the road," he yelled. "Wally, start filling in that hole."

Wally straightened up over the controls of his front-loader, gave the guy in the white hat a two-fingered salute, and revved the engine. The front-loader pivoted and headed for the back of the parking lot next door where piles of dirt were mounded up.

"That's where I am!" exclaimed Abigail. "I'm near the bottom of the second pile."

"OK," said Bert. "Let's wait until they're close to you before we make our move."

Time seemed to slow down and speed up simultaneously. Wally and his front-loader seemed to be just inching along, chipping away at the mounds of earth one scoop at a time. The loads of earth were placed in the excavation just so, then smoothed back with the bucket of the front-loader.

The man in the white hat was constantly yelling at Wally. The kids couldn't hear what he was saying over the roar of the front--loader engine. But they knew he was telling Wally to hurry-up.

Two hours passed in minutes. It was already four o'clock in the morning. The second pile of earth was about half-gone.

"Let's go," Bert said. With the pent-up energy of a two-hour wait, the kids burst from their hiding place, ran across the road and through the parking lot, and took up positions directly in front of the earth pile.

Abigail stood on top of the diminished mound that

still covered her body.

Wally finished smoothing a bucket load of fill in the hole, spun the front-loader around on its axis and headed back to the end of the parking lot. He saw was four kids with their elbows linked, standing between him and the pile of dirt.

Wally rubbed his eyes, thinking that strange things appear at four in the morning, especially when you haven't slept since yesterday morning. He took his hand away from his eyes and looked again. They were still there.

He stopped his machine half-way through the parking lot and stood up for a better view over the front of it. They were still there. Finally convinced that he wasn't hallucinating, he throttled back the engine, cupped his hands, and yelled, "Hey Mike!"

The guy in the white hat ran toward him, screaming at the top of his lungs, "What now?"

Wally pointed at the group blocking his way.

Mike ran up to them. He stood directly in front of Bert, fists clenched at his sides, and bellowed, "What do you think you're doing?"

Mike's frothing anger was scarey, but Bert stood his ground. "Stopping you," he said stammering.

The others in the human chain, quaked with fear, but held their positions.

Mike turned around to Wally, raised his right hand in the air, and made a twirling motion with it.

"Run 'em over," he yelled.

With a roar and a belch of black smoke the Caterpillar front-loader inched toward them. Closer and closer it came, its huge bucket yawning like a whale's mouth.

Then the bucket came crashing to the ground with a thunderous sound and started scraping toward Bert, Emma, Ronnie, and Derek.

Wally saw them resolutely holding to their line. Then he saw what looked like a fifth kid standing on top of the pile of dirt.

Bert and the others heard the rat-a-tat-tat of the drum and the voice of Abigail calling out, "Steady now, soldiers. Steady. Steady."

That fifth kid was in full Union uniform, every brass button polished to a high luster, every bit of leather burnished to a glow. Both hands were raised high. The drummer was drumming constant support to the steadfast line in front of him.

Derek, Ronnie, Emma, and Bert grasped each other's hands in a death grip as the font loader loomed nearer and nearer. It was now three feet away and closing, scraping along the ground. They squeezed their eyes shut and held their positions, the drumming sounding in their ears.

With less than a foot separating them from the 20-ton machine, it ground to a halt.

Wally saw another person on the mound. This one was wearing a ragged Confederate uniform and no shoes. The skin appeared to be rotting away from his maggoty face, and a grin was splashed across it. He opened his mouth and gave out a horrendous howl. Wally became the first person in nearly 150 years to hear the fabled rebel yell.

Wally jerked the machine into reverse and it skittered half-way across the lot. Then he jumped from the front-loader and ran away, gibbering and waving his arms at Mike.

"What now?" Mike roared.

Wally couldn't speak. He just pointed at the end of the lot and whimpered.

"Damn! If I want anything done here, I guess I'll just have to do it myself," Mike bellowed, climbing onto the front-loader.

As he reached for the controls, he noticed that there were now more kids there. One of them was playing a drum. No matter. They'd scatter as soon as he moved the machine forward.

Mike tried to push the lever that allowed the front-loader to go forward, but his burly arm couldn't move.

Something was terribly wrong. He felt an icy vise close over his arm. A large young man was standing in the cab of the front-loader with him, stopping him from moving the lever. This man wore a Union uniform with sergeant's stripes on the sleeve. Mike noticed two other things about him: his chest was riddled with bullet holes and he was nearly transparent.

Mixed in with the rebel yell and the beat of the drum was one word, mouthed by this apparition: "Stop."

Bert heard Abigail yell, "You tell 'em, Sergeant Ben!"

Derek added his voice to Jesse's rebel yell. Ronnie and Emma joined in as well. The morning air carried it over the entire construction area.

Mike climbed down off the front-loader and ran to the other construction workers, who had gathered at the end of the parking lot to watch the confrontation.

"Come on, men. We gonna let a couple of kids stop

us? Let's just pick 'em up and carry 'em out of our way!"

Ten men wearing hard hats and reflective vests figuratively rolled up their sleeves and moved as one unit toward the youngsters.

The kids were terrified, but to a person, they thought what it must've felt to be Abigail or Jesse facing not a handful of construction workers but an entire regiment of riflemen.

Derek tossed the hair out of his eyes and planted his feet as though he were a California redwood. Ronnie and Emma locked elbows and set their faces into expressions of indefatigable resolution. Bert took up a fighter's stance, ready to fight to the last, even if all he had were his fists.

When the two groups were fifteen feet apart, a swirl of mist appeared between them. If the road workers noticed it, they didn't show it. They came on. The mist coalesced into two lines of Confederate soldiers. The front line had its bayonet-equipped rifles and muskets lowered to waist height. The second row held theirs to their shoulders, ready to fire.

The center of the line was held by Jesse, splendid in his uniform as it looked on its very best day.

Standing right behind him, with his hand on Jesse's shoulder was another young man who looked a lot like Jesse. He was wearing a Confederate officer's uniform with captain's bars. Brothers, and not only in arms.

Abigail was standing on the mound of earth, beating away at her drum for all she was worth.

The construction gang slowed to a stop and milled about. A few of them looked over their shoulders to the big machines that represented refuge. What they saw caused their courage to evaporate. Behind them was a full company of Union soldiers in battle regalia. One man in sergeant's stripes carrying the flag and screamed support to the others. "For Abigail!" he yelled as they began their charge.

"For Abigail!" Jesse yelled in agreement, as the Confederate line closed on the construction workers.

As the Blue and Gray lines converged, the construction workers escaped to right and left.

All but Big Mike. He raised his fist and yelled that he wasn't afraid of no ghosts, he had a job to finish. At that instant, the morning was split by the wail of a police cruiser's siren as it rolled into the parking lot.

CHAPTER 12

I GOT IT!

The mist vanished, along with all the soldiers.

The four young people were still standing in front of the dirt pile. Mike was still standing over Bert, his huge fist cocked and ready to let go.

"My, my, my. What have we here?" boomed Officer Hanlon.

He placed himself directly between Bert and Big Mike, swinging his nightstick. "Having a bit of an argument with these children, are we?" he asked conversationally.

"These damn kids are ruining this job. They oughta be in jail. They just cost me an entire day's progress. I got $80,000 worth of asphalt just sitting there, a half dozen pieces of equipment idle, and an entire paving crew scattered all over the place!"

"Uh-huh," replied Officer Hanlon. "Just where is your paving crew?"

Big Mike grew even more apoplectic. His face darkened and a purple vein in his temple throbbed.

He took his ever-present unlit cigar from his mouth and threw it as far as he could before replying.

"These damn kids scared 'em away!"

With perfect aplomb, Officer Hanlon asked, "Just how did these *kids* do that?"

Big Mike tried. He really tried. But all that came out of his mouth was gibberish. He said something about being surrounded by dozens of soldiers with rifles. About some guy standing on top of the dirt pile waving a sword while a kid stood beside him beating on a drum. Some other guy was behind him waving a flag and calling him names.

"I understand," said Officer Hanlon, even though he didn't. "You're a bit worked up. What do you say we take a walk over to my car, where you can relax while I question these kids?"

He grabbed Big Mile's arm and escorted him to the police car. Big Mike climbed into the back seat without protest, still mumbling about drums, flags, rifles, and even something about horses.

Officer Hanlon removed his walkie-talkie from his gun belt and spoke into it. "Car 104 1020 at the construction site. I could use a bit of back-up here, but it's no emergency. There is one possible 302 Involuntary Commitment in custody and we'll be speaking with witnesses."

"10-4. Anything else?" the little speaker crackled.

"10-4. Dig out my Form 1 from yesterday about those kids I caught trespassing. Call their parents and tell them their kids are in custody again."

Officer Hanlon headed back to the end of the parking lot. The kids still stood arm in arm, blocking the dirt pile. Halfway there he stopped, pulled out his walkie-talkie again and said into it, "104 to radio. Better send an ambulance too. I'll probably need it for that 302."

As he approached, Abigail appeared beside Bert and pleaded, "I'm only a little ways under the dirt at the back of the pile. Come on around back. I'll show you. We're running out of time!"

Bert scrambled around to the back of the pile and started scrabbling at the dirt and rocks with his bare hands.

"No, Bert, not there. Over there!" Abigail pointed to a different place in the pile.

Bert heard more police cars arriving. Doors opened and shut, and the newly arrived police officers hurried to Officer Hanlon.

"Come on, Bert," Jesse urged, "Dig!"

"Glad you guys got here so fast."Officer Hanlon's voice rose over the morning sounds. "Tom, watch these three for me. Diane, come with me. One of them took off around the back of this pile."

Bert was on his knees digging with his bare hands for all he was worth, throwing dirt here and there and pitching the bigger rocks any which way, just so they were out of the growing hole.

The two officers walked around the dirt pile and watched him for a few seconds with astonishment. They saw neither Abigail nor Jesse, but they felt the sense of urgency in the air.

Officer Diane Russo stood still a bit, then looked over to Officer Hanlon and observed, "Kid sure is determined, isn't he?

"Yeah," agreed Officer Hanlon, "Let's get 'im out of there."

They grabbed hold of Bert's feet and started dragging him.

"Noooo," he screamed, struggling like a wildcat.

The officers grabbed him around the waist and dragged him to the front of the dirt pile.

Another set of car doors slammed, followed shortly by the worried voices of parents wondering what was going on.

Bert looked down at his bloodied fingers with all the nails broken and ragged, wondering if he could even dig anymore. He was still being held around the waist by Officer Hanlon, but his struggles were becoming less and less forceful as the energy drained from him.

Jesse and Abigail stood directly in front of the group of kids that were under the watchful eyes of the police officers.

Abigail's face was stained with tears. She cried out, "Oh Bert, only a couple of more inches to go."

Shannon O'Neill reached out to Emma as the Griffins rushed toward the group.

Bert's dad's voice boomed over everything, "What the hell is going on?"

This display of anger distracted the police officers who thought he might start a physical alteration. That distraction was all that the kids needed.

Emma, Ronnie, and Derek broke away from the adults, ran around the dirt pile, and dived for the hole Bert had enlarged.

The three of them used their hands as shovels, picks, and pry bars. Dirt and rocks cascaded from the hole in every direction.

Two soldiers in Civil War uniforms stood off to one side. The one in blue had a drum slung over the shoulder. The one in gray carried a rifle at port arms. They both shouted exhortations that only those involved in the frantic digging could hear.

One after another, starting with Emma, the kids were pulled away from the hole, struggling and screaming all the while. All of them, fingers bleeding from the digging and tears streaking their faces, were taken to the other end of the parking lot where police officers as well as their parents confronted them.

A ambulance sat sideways at the entrance to the parking lot. The EMTs were tending to Big Mike, wrapping his head in cold compresses and talking to him soothingly.

He saw the kids, ripped the compresses from his head and neck, struggled up from his sitting position, and tried to reach them, screaming at the top of his lungs that he was going to kill them all.

He didn't get far. The EMTs and one of the officers tackled him and strapped him to the stretcher.

The ambulance driver approached Officer Hanlon and said, "We'd better take this guy to the hospital. I'll radio for another unit to come check out the kids."

"OK," Officer Hanlon replied, he returned to the group which now included children, parents, police officers and members of the paving crew who had started straggling back.

Officer Hanlon asked, "OK kids, what in the Sam Hill is going on?"

Heather Griffin interrupted, her voice rising, "Oh, no. My children aren't going to say anything until their hands are looked to. They are bleeding!"

She seemed on the edge of hysteria. Shannon O'Neill placed her arms around Heather's shoulders and said calmly voice, "It's OK. I think all they really need is some soap, water and Band-Aids."

Abigail took this opportunity to walk straight through Bert's dad, who shivered uncontrollably. She placed herself directly in front of Bert and said, "Thanks Bert. I know you did everything you could. Maybe some other time."

With that, she started fading from Bert's view. Jesse put both his hands on Bert's shoulders, and for the second time that night, the rebel yell was heard on the Gettysburg battlefield. Bert felt it well up through his lungs and cascade through his throat and mouth, stunning all those around him.

Jesse called out, "Charge!"

Bert broke loose, wheeled, and ran for the dirt pile keeping up that haunting wail everyone trailing behind him

He dived head-first for the hole scrabbling like a demented dog uncovering a bone.

Just as his father (the fastest of the adults) grasped his belt, Bert stopped digging. He straightened up and held a small piece of gray cloth aloft bellowing, "I got it!"

CHAPTER 13

A MILITARY FUNERAL

It was the anniversary of the first day of the Battle of Gettysburg, July 1.

Tens of thousands of people roamed all over the battlefield. Down at Devil's Den, unsupervised children were clambering all over the boulders where dozens of soldiers had perished those many years ago. People climbed the steps to the top of Longstreet's Tower just to say they'd done it. The visitor's center was jammed with hordes of humanity buying souvenirs of all types. Kids strutted through town proudly wearing both Union and Confederate kepis. Traffic was at a near stand still, bumper to bumper all along the Chambersburg Pike. Where once drums, bugles, musket fire, and cannon shot roared, now horns bleated as impatient drivers sought to turn onto Seminary Ridge just so they could say they'd done that, too.

In the town of Gettysburg, the sidewalks thronged with people sipping cold drinks and eating soft-serve ice cream cones. Every air-conditioned space in the town was filled with people trying to escape the July heat.

There were at least as many people in town this day as there had been on that day in 1863. The difference was that nobody was dying here today, not even from the heat.

A group of people gathered at a freshly-dug grave within the Gettysburg National Cemetery.

A small flag-draped coffin sat beside the grave. A full U.S. Army color guard stood at attention at the head of the grave, bearing the flags of the United States of America, the United States Army, the Commonwealth of Pennsylvania, and the 143rd Pennsylvania Volunteers.

A representative from the governor's office was there in full diplomatic dress, including the top hat that he held over his chest.

One of the color guard removed the flag from the coffin, folded it, and handed it over to a representative of the 143rd Pennsylvania Volunteers.

An Army colonel placed Bronze Star, Purple Heart,

and Civil War Campaign medals on the coffin which was then lowered into the grave. A bugle sounded taps as a muffled drum thumped a dirge. The color guard saluted. A rifle squad fired volleys.

Bert, Ronnie, Emma, and Derek stood at the edge of the grave, tears streaming down their faces. A pretty blond girl went to them one at a time and kissed them on the forehead. When she got to Bert, she gave him a big hug as well. As she faded from sight, she mouthed the words, "thank you" over and over again.

Each person at the graveside dribbled a handful of dirt onto the coffin as they paid their last respects.

A young man wearing a long gray overcoat, and carrying a musket in his left hand waved good-bye to the four children and walked right into a tree.

Then the O'Neill and Griffin families left the graveyard. As they gathered around their cars to return to the campground, Bert asked, "Dad, can we go to Fredricksburg next year for vacation?"

Emma looked at him quizzically.

All he said was "Jesse."

She understood.

The End

ABOUT THE AUTHOR

Ed Kelemen is a writer, columnist, and playwright who lives in a small West Central Pennsylvania town with his wife, two of five sons, a trio of humongous dogs and a clutch of attitude-ridden cats. His article and short stories have appeared in numerous local, regional, and national publications. Visit with him at www.ekelemen.com.

PS: Ed wants to know if you can figure out what's wrong with one of the graphics that are at the front of each chapter. If you figure it out, email him at ed@ekelemen.com.

Made in the USA
Las Vegas, NV
13 March 2024

87132704R00066